West 7th Street Series

BUSINESS
As Usual

David Haynes

SUMMIT
BOOKS

Perfection Learning®

Illustrator: Laura J. Bryant
Book design: Kay Ewald

About the Author

David Haynes has worked as a classroom teacher and
as a teacher-in-residence for the National Board for
Professional Teaching Standards. He is the author of
The Gumma Wars (Perfection Learning, 2001), *Retold
African American Folktales* (Perfection Learning, 1997),
Live at Five (Milkweed Editions, 1996), *Heathens* (New
Rivers Press, 1996), *Somebody Else's Mama* (Milkweed
Editions, 1995), and *Right by My Side* (New Rivers
Press, 1993), a novel that won the 1992 Minnesota
Voices Project and was selected by the American Library
Association as one of the best books for young adults of
1994. His short stories have been published in journals
and anthologies, and two were read and recorded for
National Public Radio's "Selected Shorts." *Granta*
Magazine selected him as one of America's best young
novelists in 1996.

For information, contact
Perfection Learning® Corporation
1000 North Second Avenue, P.O. Box 500
Logan, Iowa 51546-0500.
Phone: 800-831-4190 • Fax: 712-644-2392

Paperback ISBN 0-7891-5413-7
Cover Craft® ISBN 0-7569-0071-9
Printed in the U.S.A.

Table of Contents

A Certain Person

MY NAME IS Bobby Samson. This story is about economics and the West 7th Wildcats and Kevin Olsen and how sometimes what you think about people and what is real can be two very different things.

There are six of us Wildcats—me, Lu, Tou Vue, Kevin, Johnny Vang, and Tony R. We're not a gang. We just all live near West 7th Street in St. Paul and are best friends.

All of us Wildcats think our sixth-grade teacher is really cool. That's a good thing because there is only one sixth-grade teacher at River Road School, and, therefore, if you don't like Mr. Harrison, you are pretty much out of luck for a whole year.

April is the time for Mr. Harrison's end-of-the-year special: his spring economics unit. Kids at River Road wait for six years to be a part of it, and it is well worth the wait. You can believe that.

Mr. Harrison is funny and smart, and the boys get along with him pretty well. He is the sort of teacher who, when all of his students do their projects and are nice to one another, declares an all-day recess and takes the class out to the playground and lets them have fun. The smart part is that Mr. Harrison knows

5

that even the hardiest players—which the Wildcats most definitely are—get tired of all-day recess by about 11:30, and that by lunchtime, with one or two exceptions, most of the kids are begging to come inside and do something else. Have a spelling test. Do math problems. Anything else, please.

Kevin Olsen—a.k.a. the wildest of the Wildcats—is the one big exception. Boy, can that guy play games! Just point him to a playground or field, and he is ready to go. It doesn't matter much to Kevin what the game is, as long as it involves some kind of running or jumping or hopping or moving around. Throw in a ball—any kind of ball—and he is in his version of heaven. He plays catch, baseball, softball, football, soccer, tennis, capture the flag, combat, badminton, volleyball, freeze tag, stoop tag, electric tag, king of the hill, kickball, lawn bowling, and tumbling. If none of the Wildcats want to play, he will cross the field and get into a game of red rover with the little guys.

And when Kevin really gets desperate, he can even be found smack-dab in the middle of a bunch of girls playing jump rope. Just imagine—Kevin on one end and Jenny Pederson, the Wildcats' archenemy, on the other, turning double Dutch. Or Kevin in the middle, jumping away and singing with a big grin on his face. The girls, for some reason no one can figure out, always let him play. He actually likes playing with them and never cares what anyone else thinks.

When the whistle blows to come inside, most of the kids get in line right away. The Wildcats are sometimes the last ones, but we are almost always in line before Mr. Harrison opens the door to let us in. Opening the door is the signal that if you aren't already lined up, you might end up on the tardy list, which means you'll be sitting out the first five minutes of the next recess.

Kevin's name has a permanent place on the top of that tardy list. He never lines up in time. You can never count on him to be in the starting lineup for the next game because he is always sitting against that wall, where the late kids have to wait out their time. He's always waving and cheering as if he were in the stands at the Twins game at the Metrodome.

I guess you could say that Kevin is more or less Mr. Harrison's problem child. In a room full of 30 normal 12-year-old boys and girls, Kevin is the one who stands out. The one who stands out in the hall, that is.

Take today, for example. After our bathroom break, Mr. Harrison had just gotten us settled down for reading time.

Reading time is after lunch when Mr. Harrison reads to us from a book he chooses from the library. Now, you wouldn't think a bunch of sixth graders would sit still when being read to, but Mr. Harrison has great taste in books and is a very dramatic reader. He has a whole bunch of different voices he uses to let you know when different characters are speaking, and during the exciting parts, his voice gets excited too. A lot of us just put our heads down and get carried away in the story.

Today Mr. Harrison was reading from *Hatchet*, a real exciting story about a boy who gets stuck out in the woods after a plane crash. The boy sounds like he could be one of the Wildcats.

"Who would like to catch us up on where we left off yesterday?" Mr. Harrison asked.

"Me! Me!" Johnny Vang yelled, waving his hand.

"Go ahead, John," Mr. Harrison offered. Mr. Harrison is probably the only person on earth who doesn't call Johnny Vang *Johnny Vang*.

"That big moose got him," Johnny Vang said.

"Yeah, a big moose," some of the other boys agreed.

"Anything else?" Mr. Harrison asked.

"Yeah, this," said Kevin, and he let out a big long belch full of all the air he'd swallowed out at the drinking fountain during bathroom break for just this purpose.

We tried not to laugh, but you know how it is in sixth grade. What could be funnier than a big loud belch from the class goofball? We didn't laugh too much, though, because of the look on Mr. Harrison's face. He had on his disgusted and frustrated look.

"I know, I know," said Kevin, shaking his mop of blond hair around his head and heading for his seat in the hall. He staggered to the front of the room as if his legs had fallen asleep.

"Sorry," he said, as he traipsed past Mr. Harrison, but you could tell from the way his eyes were shining that he probably wasn't too sorry. Mr. Harrison didn't even look at him but instead aimed that same disgusted and frustrated look at the rest of us.

"This late in the year," he said, "I'd think we'd all know not to encourage a certain person." He said this after "a certain person" was already seated out in the hallway. I'll bet we all felt a lot sorrier than "a certain person" did. From anywhere in the room you could hear him out there, scratching his back against the wall like an old cat, trying to get comfortable.

The deal was that as long as "a certain person" didn't make faces in the door and try to get more attention for himself, Mr. Harrison would leave the door open so that Kevin could hear the reading. Despite his antics, Kevin enjoys a good story as much as the next person.

Things like the belching incident have been going on all year. Mr. Harrison has tried to be patient, but with Kevin there is always a new trick. It has been this way for as long as any of the Wildcats can remember. Since kindergarten according to Lu, who has known Kevin the longest. Teachers have tried everything—sending him to the principal's office, giving him after-school detention, having him meet with the social worker. Kevin's poor mom has been called into the office so many times that she decided to volunteer at school part-time.

"As long as I have to be there every day," she tells people.

But what can she do, really? Kevin is . . . Kevin, after all. Everybody knows that. He is just one of those kids who happens to come with a lot of extra life in him. He is the one who can make his face into a thousand silly shapes and twist his body around to match them. He is the one who knows the good jokes, even the ones you probably wouldn't want your parents to hear, and he remembers the punch lines too. He is the one who brings the best gift to the party, and the one who knows the best practical jokes—like the rattlesnake seeds in the envelope—and the one who always gets you to fall for them, even if you've seen them before. He is always laughing and smiling.

Okay, I guess you could say he is more or less a knucklehead, but he isn't a stupid one. In fact, Kevin does just as well in most subjects as the rest of us sixth graders, which is probably the reason Ms. Filipek-Johnson, our principal, doesn't throw him out. The thing is, school just isn't made for kids like Kevin. At school we're supposed to be quiet and never call attention to ourselves. We're supposed to raise our hands and be serious. Even a good teacher like Mr. Harrison—one who likes to laugh and tell silly jokes and have a good time—has a hard time with someone like Kevin.

"You have to draw a line, boys and girls," Mr. Harrison told us early in the school year, after Kevin had superglued Mike Caulfield's Trapper Keeper shut. "I like a good joke as much as the next person, but some people take things too far." Everyone knew that "some people" meant "a certain person." At the time "a certain person" had been picked up by his mother and was at the store replacing the Trapper Keeper. Mr. Harrison gave us a lecture about our responsibility to help "a certain person" remember to be good and to do the right thing. Most of us—the West 7th Wildcats in particular—just rolled our eyes and shook our heads.

We have basements full of flat footballs and action figures with missing parts because Kevin launched them onto someone's roof. When you have Kevin for a friend, that is part of the deal. If you want the fun, you have to put up with the trouble. We Wildcats figure it's worth it. Maybe someday the school will figure that out too.

I'll Give Anything

"GIRLS AND BOYS, today begins your great adventure in the world of big business and big finance."

This is the way Mr. Harrison started the first day of his economics unit. We couldn't believe that our turn had finally come. We were all on our best behavior, even Kevin, because no one wanted to risk being sent to the principal's office and maybe missing out on one of the really fun parts.

Mr. Harrison held up a piece of writing paper. "Here I have a brand-spanking-new sheet of blue-lined paper. Larry, how much will you pay me for this?"

"Nothing," Lu said. (His name is Larry Underwood, but we call him "Lu.")

"Why not? It's perfectly clean. No wrinkles. You like paper, don't you?"

"I've got a whole pad of paper," Lu said, holding up his notebook.

"Let's say you're almost out of paper. Would you buy it from me then?"

"No. I'd just get some from Tony R."

"Not from me," Tony R said. "You buy your own paper, boy."

"Then Moms will buy me some."

"How about these?" Mr. Harrison held up a packet of green hall passes. You need a hall pass at River Road for everything—to go to the bathroom, to go to the office if your dad picks you up, practically to breathe. "I'll even sign every single one for you. You can have free run of the school!"

"I'll take 'em!" Kevin's hand shot up. He looked like he did when the Wildcats went to the all-you-can-eat pizza buffet, like he was going to drool. He jumped out of his seat.

"Not so fast, Buster. What'll you give me for them?"

"Uh . . . uh . . ." He felt around in his pockets. "I got a quarter!"

"I'll take it!" Mr. Harrison said. He started to walk back toward Kevin to trade him the passes for the money.

"Just a sec," said Jenny Pederson. She fished two

coins from her hip pack. "I'll give you 30 cents."

Mr. Harrison changed course. "Apparently I priced these too low," he said.

Kevin groaned as if someone were stepping on his toes. "No! Please! I'll give you 25 cents and five Twins rookie cards."

"Those wouldn't happen to be the rookie cards I told you to leave at home and never bring back, would they?" Mr. Harrison asked.

Kevin, as usual, was fast with a story. "Uh . . . these are different ones. These I . . . uh . . . just found on the way to school today. Honest." We Wildcats looked at one another and rolled our eyes. Good old Kevin.

"Let me see," Mr. Harrison said, thinking out loud. "I don't really like baseball cards, but I'll bet I could trade those to someone else for something I do want. Or maybe I could . . ."

"Here," said Jenny Pederson. "Fifty cents. Cash."

"Sold," said Mr. Harrison. Jenny strolled back to her desk, flipping her pad of passes in everyone's face. Kevin curled up his lip at her. We hoped he'd calm down before recess.

"Uh-oh," Mr. Harrison said. "Now, here's an interesting development." He removed a small box from his closet. He proceeded to walk up and down the rows of the classroom, handing a pad of green passes to everyone.

He kept one for himself, which he held up in front

of us. "What will you give me for these now?"

The whole class laughed at him.

"I don't get it," he said. "A minute ago, I had people fighting over this same item." He made one of his funny faces, and then he took the box that the passes had been in over to Jenny Pederson's desk. He returned her 50 cents and asked her to collect the pads of passes.

"I've got one more item," he said. He opened his wallet and pulled out what looked like two tickets. "These are tickets to the NCAA Final Four to be held right here at the Target Center. What will you give me for these?"

Everyone thought Tony R was going to have a heart attack. He gasped and crawled on his knees up to Mr. Harrison.

"Anything. I'll be your servant for the rest of my life," he said.

Tony R, as you can probably figure, is the world's biggest sports fan. Basketball is his all-time favorite thing. He would die for those tickets, but some others of us would too.

"I'll give you a hundred dollars," one kid yelled.

"I'll give you a million," said another.

"I'll give you my baby sister," said still a third.

Mr. Harrison sighed. "Sorry, guys." He opened his wallet and put the tickets back inside. "There isn't enough money in the world to get me to sell these tickets."

"Not even for a million dollars?" Tou Vue asked.

Mr. Harrison rubbed his chin for a minute. "Bring in the money first. Then we'll talk." He waved two fingers across the room like a magic wand—his signal that we were to settle down again.

"What we've just experienced, boys and girls, is called the law of supply and demand. If I have something that everybody wants," he held up a pad of passes, "I can charge a lot of money for it. But if everybody already has plenty," he held up the whole box of passes, "then I might as well give them away."

I raised my hand. "Let's say you have something everybody wants, but nobody has any money?" The other Wildcats snickered. My mom used to be in the Navy, and she is always complaining that money is tighter than a seal on a submarine door.

"Excellent question, Robert. What does everybody think?"

"You could sell it cheaper," Lu guessed.

Jenny Pederson sputtered at him. "You could lose money too."

"Jenny's got you there, Larry. You can't sell it any cheaper than it cost you to make. Otherwise you'll go out of business."

Johnny Vang raised his hand. "You could help people get jobs so that they would have money to buy your stuff."

"You mean a business could help people get jobs?"

Mr. Harrison asked. "Is that what businesses do? Help people get jobs?"

"Businesses," said Jenny Pederson in her snootiest voice, "exist to make money."

"I guess we can see who's going to be River Road's businessperson of the year," Mr. Harrison said.

The Wildcats gave one another looks that said over our dead bodies she would. That dumb Jenny Pederson.

Jenny's been making trouble for the Wildcats ever since her family moved in next to Tony R's back in the third grade. She has to be the best at everything. She has to play in every game, and she always has to be captain and make the rules. She hates it that the West 7th Wildcats is a boys-only club. She is always doing things like throwing stink bombs into the clubhouse we have in my backyard, or making prank phone calls when we have a sleepover party. It's hard to get even with her too. She is one of those people who, every time you think you have a plan to get back at her, turns out to be one step ahead of you. Try to ambush her with water balloons and you find out she has a whole arsenal of super-powered squirt guns ready to go.

"Well, what do you know?" Mr. Harrison said, taking out his wallet again. "I just happened to come across another set of tickets here."

Tony R started gasping again and was almost to his knees.

"Hang on, Antonio. They're good, but they're not that good. Thanks to a generous donation from our parents' group, I do have some tickets to Valleyfair."

A bunch of us cheered. Valleyfair is almost the best place you can go on a nice summer day, with the water rides and the Wild Thing roller coaster.

"Slow down! You know me by now. I don't just give prizes away for nothing. There's another principle in economics called *motivation*. Why do I come to work every day?"

" 'Cause you're crazy!" Kevin said in his goofiest voice. We all laughed.

"Come to think of it, a person would have to be pretty crazy to put up with you guys," Mr. Harrison said, which just caused the rest of us to laugh even more.

"But can anyone really guess why I come to work every day? Tou Vue looks like a man with an answer."

"Because you get paid," Tou Vue said.

"Absolutely. Now, don't get me wrong. I love my job and I enjoy you kids a lot, but just like everyone else, I've got to have an incentive. Something that *I* want. Likewise, I'm going to give *you* an incentive for the economics unit. The team with the most successful project—as judged by our very own principal, Ms. Filipek-Johnson—will win tickets to Valleyfair. But even if your team doesn't win, you can make real money. You want to know why?"

We all nodded eagerly.

"I'll tell you tomorrow," he said. We moaned.

"First, let me tell you about tonight's assignment."

WEST 7TH ST.

A Million Dollars

TONIGHT'S ASSIGNMENT WAS every kid's dream. Sometimes a kid can go through an entire life waiting for a chance like this. We were going to fulfill one of the biggest fantasies of all time.

Tonight's assignment was to give our parents a test!

"I've got another important tip from the business world," Mr. Harrison said as he passed around the test papers. "It will help make sure you do a good job on this assignment. Kevin, what do you do when you want your mom to give you some money to go to the movies?"

"He just goes into her purse and takes it," Tony R said. We got a big laugh out of that.

"Shut up! I do not." Kevin looked really irritated.

"I wasn't speaking to you, Antonio. And 'shut up' remains, as always, on our embargoed-phrase list. Continue, Kevin."

"Sorry," Kevin said. "With my mom, you have to wait until she's real happy about something, and then you kind of have to, you know, snuggle up to her and let her rub your head and stuff. Then if you ask real nice, she might give you some money."

"Cute," said Mr. Harrison. "Anybody else?"

Lu said, "For my mom and dad, you have to wait until they're running around like crazy getting ready for work or to go to a party or something. When they're really not paying attention, you spring it on them."

"Sounds a little underhanded to me."

"Yeah, but it's fun," laughed Lu.

"You want some money from my mom, you got to scrub down the head," I said. *Head* is Navy talk for the bathroom.

"You've got to work to eat," Mr. Harrison said. "Your mom sounds like my dad. Okay, the tip is, you have to understand your audience to get what you want. It's called *marketing*. And what do you want? You want your parents to take this test, but you've got to give it to them at the right time."

I could tell Johnny Vang and Tou Vue, being Hmong, would have a particular problem with the assignment. Their families have been in this country only a little while. Neither of Tou Vue's parents speak much English, and Johnny Vang's parents are learning English at night school. Mr. Harrison forgets sometimes that some of the things he sends home don't make any sense to them. Either that or it's a problem he doesn't know how to fix. He doesn't speak Hmong, after all, or Russian, either. We have some Russian kids in our class too. He probably thinks that sixth graders are old enough to go home and help their parents, and that's what Johnny Vang and Tou Vue did.

The next morning before school, we Wildcats compared notes on the assignment. Here's what happened when we tested our parents.

"I don't know any of these words," Tou Vue's mother told him. He had asked her the vocabulary part of the test.

"What about *price*? Like what things cost over at the grocery."

"Oh, yes," his dad said. "Tell your teacher we did things very differently back in our country."

Tou Vue's dad went on to tell him how in Laos, which is the country Tou Vue's family came from, the Hmong families depended on the crops they grew.

"We grew all our own food and hunted and fished. If you wanted something that you couldn't grow, if your grandmother wanted a special kind of fabric to sew, we would trade with someone who had that."

"So you didn't have a job?"

His father and mother laughed.

"Every day you worked. So you could live. But it was not like here."

Johnny Vang's dad and mom were very excited to see the test.

"We are studying the same things!" his father

exclaimed. Johnny's parents are in school to learn everything they need to know about how to open their own business. Mr. Vang has learned to repair cars, and he wants to open his own garage.

"Tell your teacher he has misspelled *inventory*," Mrs. Vang instructed.

At first Lu's parents were excited to be working on a family project together.

"Let's see," Lu's dad said. " 'Define *inflation*.' " He wrote down an answer and passed it to Lu's mother to read.

" 'Inflation is when businesses have to slow things down because they've made too much.' " his mother read. "Wrong!"

"I beg your pardon," said Mr. Underwood.

"What you've described, my dear, is a recession," said Mrs. Underwood.

"I don't think so," said her husband.

I pictured Lu's head bouncing back and forth from one parent to the other. Sometimes his parents' bickering makes him sad, but a lot of times they can be kind of funny. Moms, as he calls her, has medium-brown skin like he does, while his dad's skin is a rich brown color. Lu likes being an only child most of the time. Except when it is time to do homework.

"Let's move on, shall we," his father continued. " 'What would you do if you won a million dollars in the lottery?' Wow! What would we do, Larry?"

"Buy me a car!" Lu said.

"And you can drive me right to Florida," said his dad.

His mother wrinkled her brow. "Honey, you know that hot weather gives me heat bumps." She stared off into the distance dreamily. "A nice condo in Aspen where I could go skiing with the movie stars . . . "

"All that cold weather and snow, woman. We might as well stay here."

"It's my million dollars too," she said. "I should have a say on where we spend it."

"Well, I bought the winning ticket," his dad answered.

"Where does it say that? Larry, where does it say that this is your father's money?"

"I say we're going to Florida."

"Aspen."

"Florida."

"Aspen."

"Florida."

Lu told us that just about then he snuck off and started playing Nintendo.

Mr. Rodriguez had just gotten in from his shift on the police force when Tony R gave him the test. "If I had a million dollars . . ." Tony R's father wrote, "I would first of all send my son, Antonio, to tennis camp." He handed his answer to Tony R. "How is that, Antonio?"

"Couldn't it be basketball camp?"

"We've got a million dollars. Why not both?" Mr. Rodriguez replied.

"Fine by me."

"Both it is." His father continued writing.

Tony R likes these times at the end of the day when his dad comes home. His father always spends time with him after he tucks Tony's little sisters into bed. Sometimes they watch TV together or play a game of cards. Tony R thinks his dad works too hard, and he worries about him out there in his squad car. Sometimes he is afraid that something will happen to his dad, that maybe a criminal will shoot at him, but his dad assures him that mostly his job is helping people and talking to kids.

"And I would set some money aside to feed people who are hungry," his father wrote. This made Tony R very happy. If he had a million dollars, he told the Wildcats, he would buy his dad a shiny badge made out of 100-percent gold.

" 'Explain how a bank makes money,' " my mom read. "I'll tell you how a bank makes money. They make it by cheating hard-working women like me, that's how they make it."

I was amazed. Every question seemed to make my

mother more excited than the last. I played Candyland on the table with my little brother, Donald—we call him Alf—while Momma worked on the test.

"Just the other day, for example, I go to the bank to cash your father's check—a perfectly good military-issue check drawn on the full faith and credit of the United States government—and the teller tells me I can't have 50 dollars back until the check clears. I said to the man, 'Excuse me, sir. If this check isn't any good, then there isn't a check in this entire bank that's any good.' And he says to me, 'It's policy ma'am.' 'Bilgewater!' I said to him. I'll give him policy. They had better not look at me cross-eyed the next time I go to that bank."

I think Momma will lose her mind over money someday. I have no idea how our family is doing as far as money goes, because other than complain every time she has to open her wallet, Momma doesn't say. We have plenty of food and plenty of clothes. I just keep my mouth closed and hope my dad comes home from his ship soon. Momma is great, but it's nice to have a dad around too.

Momma read the next question. " 'Do you have a plan to get rich?' Do I have a plan to get rich? I'll tell you mates something: if I had a plan to get rich . . ."

Just then Alf landed in the gumdrop forest and was squealing, so I didn't pay attention to her answer.

And as for Kevin, well, leave it to Kevin to be the one who "lost" his assignment sheet.

The next day in class, Mr. Harrison called on us to report our parents' answers. All of us were excited to share. Some of the answers were pretty funny, and a lot of parents had very different ideas. Then Mr. Harrison called on Kevin.

"What did your mom have to say, Kevin?" Mr. Harrison asked.

Kevin shrugged.

"What? You can't read her writing?"

He shrugged again. "Didn't do it," he said softly.

"Okay," Mr. Harrison said. He made a mark in his grade book and moved on to the next person. You could tell he was unhappy, though. Everyone had done the work except Kevin.

After we took turns, Mr. Harrison gave us the next weird assignment. "And now, you must grade your parents' papers."

We started cheering and sat up in eager anticipation of the answer sheets. Instead he brought out a box of books.

"You'll find the answers in here and in the dictionaries, and you'll find a bit of information in the encyclopedias. Get started right away, please, so we can have some time to talk about the big project. Kevin, I want to see you in the hall."

Dum-de-dum-dum, we all thought. Just like on *Dragnet* on *Nickelodeon*. We knew what was going on out in that hall. Most of us had been there at one time or another.

"Do you have an explanation?" we overheard Mr. Harrison ask Kevin.

"Please, don't shrug," he continued. "We've already talked about that. You're a young man now and young men answer questions. Do you have an explanation?"

"No, sir."

"This bothers me, Kevin. I thought you would like our economics unit. I thought we had a deal with your mom that you'd take your assignments home."

"I forgot," was all he could get out. I knew he was sorry he had forgotten.

Kevin forgets a lot of things. He gets home from school and his favorite show is on. Then one of us Wildcats calls on the phone and asks him to come over. And then it's suppertime, and after supper another show that he likes comes on. And another. And then it's bedtime. The next morning he gets up at dawn and shoots some hoops (which the neighbors hate). And then it's time for school again. The days go so fast. Things get away from him. Papers stay in the bottom of his backpack until it's too late.

"I guess we'll try again tomorrow," Mr. Harrison said.

We quickly began working hard. Mr. Harrison made a note on the folder he keeps on his desk for Kevin's mom. He no longer looked frustrated, only tired—like he wanted to give up.

"Can we get our projects now?" Jenny Pederson said. "Please, please, please."

"I don't know," he said. "Do you think you're ready?"

"Yes!" we all screamed.

"All right, then." He got us organized back at our desks and then prepared to pass out the instructions. Everyone's mood brightened. Even Kevin made trumpet noises through his fist.

Choosing Sides

■ ■

"YOU ARE IN business!" Mr. Harrison announced.

And that's just what the big assignment was. Mr. Harrison called it the marketplace project. But before we could get started, he wanted us to divide into groups. Which was the first sign that our class project might be a little rockier than we wanted it to be. There were only two rules for the groups—you couldn't have more than four people and you had to live close enough together to be able to get to one another's houses to work. Everybody was pretty happy with those rules, actually. Sometimes he made us work with people we weren't good friends with, and a lot of times you had to make sure there was at least one person of the opposite sex in your group. If you're slow figuring things out, that means girls. It was much more fun when you could make your own groups.

The first thing you need to understand is that the Wildcats are the best buddies in the whole world. We all live close to West 7th Street, and we spend practically all of our time together. Everyone knows that any one of us would do anything for the others—give up a turn at bat, lend five dollars, take the blame for a cracked windowpane. Anything! But now we had sort of a problem on our hands. You see, we could only have four in a group, and there were six Wildcats in Mr. Harrison's room.

"I'm sorry boys, but I'm going to have to stand firm on this one. In order for the marketplace project to work, I've got to have at least seven businesses going. That means no more than four per group. Sorry."

So we went back to our huddle. Time was running short. A couple of the other groups had already taken out their notebooks and were making plans.

"What'll we do, guys?" Lu asked. Nobody said anything. Everyone was waiting for someone else to make the first move. Finally Tou Vue got up his courage.

"I'll see you guys later," he said. "I'll go work in my cousin's group." Tou Vue has a cousin, Blia, in

Mr. Harrison's room. She's a real nice, quiet person. She and a friend were already in the corner starting on their idea. We pretended to try to talk Tou Vue out of it, but in reality, we were relieved he had made the decision. It made it that much easier on the rest of us.

"I want all groups formed within the next two minutes," Mr. Harrison announced. "We've got an ambitious schedule."

"Great," I said. "What'll we do now?"

"We could pull names out of a hat," Tony R suggested.

Everyone agreed we could do that, but you didn't see anybody rushing to get out paper to make the slips.

"What's the problem, gentlemen?" Mr. Harrison asked, circling around our group.

"Everything be cool," Johnny Vang told him. Johnny Vang likes to talk like the black kids.

"I see five bodies here," Mr. Harrison said. "I need to see a group of four and I need to see it in about 90 seconds." He looked up at the clock.

And then one of those things happened that you really can't explain, even if you were there to experience it yourself. It's like when you are in a car accident or when you fall out of the tree and break your arm. One minute things are fine, and then the next minute, for no reason anybody can say, things change.

"Here is a group of four," Lu said.

All at once, me and Lu and Tony R and Johnny Vang moved together. Kevin was left by himself. Nobody planned for that to happen. It just did.

At first Kevin sort of laughed. Then, when he saw that we were serious, his face crumpled up like a paper bag, and he ran from the room.

"Nice work, guys," Mr. Harrison said. He went after Kevin.

Nobody said anything for a minute. We felt terrible. The Wildcats had been friends forever. This was practically the worst thing that had ever happened to us.

"He'd have ruined everything," Lu said. Lu always has to say what everybody else is thinking. Even if it doesn't help. I'm the practical one. I get that from my mom. I suggested we get to work instead of sitting there feeling sorry for Kevin. So we did.

It was hard at first. We tried to concentrate, but you could just tell that everyone's mind was somewhere else. You just knew what the guys were thinking—Is this any way to treat a friend?

In a little while, Mr. Harrison opened the door and asked Jenny Pederson to come out into the hallway.

Dum-de-dum-dum, we all thought.

She stormed back into the room a minute later with her arms crossed. Kevin stormed in right behind her with his arms crossed too. They both went and sat by Tyra Allen and Kelly Lee, whom Jenny had chosen for her group. We knew what had happened. Kevin had been forced to join the enemy team!

Survey Says!

"COMIC BOOKS!"

"Corn dogs!"

"Fudge!"

"S'mores!"

The Wildcats, or at least those of us who were working on the marketplace project together, met over at Tony R's house for a brainstorming session to figure out what to sell on Marketplace Day. That's the day we turn the cafeteria into a store—a marketplace—and sell our products. You see, the general idea of the project was that you and your friends had to choose a product or service to sell, find investors, advertise your product, and be ready to sell it on Marketplace Day.

In class, right after we had chosen teams, Mr. Harrison talked with us about market research. He said that before a business opens its doors, the investors—or the people who gave the owners the money to start the business—want some proof that people actually want what the business is selling.

"I suggest you start with yourselves," Mr. Harrison said. "After all, the other customers will be boys and girls just like you."

"Chocolate! Chocolate! Chocolate!" I said. I'm

35

one of those people who can't get enough of the stuff. I'd even eat chocolate spaghetti if there were such a thing.

"We can't just sell pieces of chocolate," Lu said. "The rules say 'no retail.' "

"No retail" meant that you couldn't just buy stuff that other people had already made at a factory and turn around and sell it. Whatever you sold had to be made up of at least two things that were somehow changed by your company.

I thought about that for a minute. "We could have chocolate, and then put other things into it. Like peanuts or raisins or even bananas or strawberries."

Lu rolled his eyes. He was violating the first rule of brainstorming, which is you aren't supposed to judge other people's ideas.

"We could offer a homework service," Tony R said. "We could offer to do the homework for the younger kids for a dollar a subject. It wouldn't cost us anything. Think of how much profit we'd make!"

Profit is the money you make after you have paid your expenses. We sure could make a lot of profit running a homework service, except Ms. Filipek-Johnson and Mr. Harrison and the other teachers would probably disapprove. Besides, who wants to spend time doing more homework when we already do enough as it is.

"We could sell baseball caps," Lu suggested. Lu

loves his baseball caps. You never see him when he doesn't have a hat perched on his head—sometimes with the bill facing front, sometimes with the bill facing back.

"That's retail," Johnny Vang warned.

"Not if we change them," Lu replied. "We could get some plain hats and then make our own custom patches to iron on. Then all the kids in school could have their own personalized hats."

That was a great idea, we decided, until we thought about it and realized that not many kids at our school could afford a new hat or would want to buy one when they had a bunch of other things to choose from on Marketplace Day.

Finally, the Wildcats decided that our best bet was food. All kids like to eat. We just had to figure out what.

"The key to successful market research," Mr. Harrison told us in class, "is gathering good information. How would you go about finding out what would sell best at River Road School? Any ideas?"

Tyra raised her hand. "You could ask people questions."

"Good idea. Tell me something, Robert. Let's say you asked me what my favorite cookie was, and I told you snickerdoodles. Would you make snickerdoodles?"

"I don't even know what a snickerdoodle is," I answered, and everybody laughed. Mr. Harrison was full of words like *snickerdoodle* and *lefse*.

"It's just a plain old cookie with cinnamon and sugar. Would you make those?"

I had to think about it a minute. "I don't think so . . . I'm not sure."

"Why not?"

"You may be the only person that likes snippleloolies or whatever you said."

"Snickerdoodles. Very good, Robert. You've got to have enough information to make a good decision. That means you have to ask enough people and enough different kinds of people too."

In other words, you couldn't ask just the boys or just the girls or just the other sixth graders. Mr. Harrison gave us lots of other ideas about how to do a survey. He told us to be sure to ask how much people would be willing to pay, and he also told us it was a good idea to give people more than one idea to choose from.

"Two things to be careful of," Mr. Harrison said. "First, sometimes people don't know what they want until they see it in the store. So just because everybody tells you candy, that doesn't mean candy is what you should sell. You've got to think about a lot of other things, including what you know how to make and what you can afford. Sometimes you have to take a risk."

The second thing he warned us about was the start of the next big problem.

"Market research is very valuable. If your group

finds out something good, I wouldn't spread it around."

We decided to ask the younger kids whether they would prefer to have something sweet to eat (like cookies or brownies or candy) or something salty and crispy (like pretzels or popcorn or nachos). When it was the Wildcats' turn to go around the school, we started in the kindergarten. Boy, was that a mistake. Just mention the word *candy* and those little guys start squealing like crazy and squirming around like a bowl full of earthworms. Finally, their teacher, Miss Hannum, had to ask us to leave. She had taught most of us when we were in kindergarten and still likes us, so she was pretty nice about it.

The first and second graders were frustrating too. It wasn't until we got to the third graders that we were able to get answers to our questions. We talked to Mr. Harrison about our problem with the younger kids and he told us we were looking at it the wrong way.

"What exactly were those younger kids saying to you?" he asked us.

"Everything!" I said, and I was the least frustrated of any of us. With a little brother like Alf at home, I was used to being around those guys.

"What does 'everything' tell you?" Mr. Harrison asked.

We all smiled at the same time. Of course! As far as a lot of the younger kids were concerned, it didn't matter what we sold. They would probably eat chocolate-covered ants if we told them they were candy.

After that we concentrated on the fourth and fifth graders. We learned some interesting things. First of all, a lot of kids had friends on the other teams, and we think they were kind of lying to us to get us to pick the wrong product. Also, we found out that one of the other groups of boys was going to make nachos and that another group was going to make bracelets. Kids sure have big mouths.

We had another meeting over at Lu's house.

"Everybody likes sweet things," said Lu, and we all agreed. The only problem was we had to pick the right kind of sweet thing.

"I think it should be chocolate," I said.

"We be knowing that," said Johnny Vang. "I think we'd make more money with cookies."

"Why?" Tony R asked.

"Because chocolate costs a lot more to make. Cookies, you mix up a big bowl full of dough and you can make lots."

"Yeah, but Bobby's right," Lu said. "Everybody likes chocolate."

And then it was like everybody had the same idea at the same time. Things like that happen when you have really good friends. The idea was sitting right there in front of our faces.

Chocolate chip cookies!

Everyone agreed the idea was an absolute winner. With our homework done, we took off to play some softball over behind River Road School. Tou Vue and Kevin met us there. Kevin was in a particularly good mood. For a few days he hadn't talked to anyone but Tou Vue, but now he seemed to have forgiven us. Nobody mentioned what had happened with the marketplace groups. It was like that had never happened and we were back in the good old days.

After the game we headed toward our houses. Lu walked down Davern Street with me and Tou Vue and Johnny Vang (we live close·to one another), and Tony R and Kevin, who live across West 7th, took off down Primrose Street.

The next day in class the groups took turns reporting our research. We wanted to be last. Nobody in the Wildcats likes to talk in front of class except for Kevin, who wasn't on our team, of course. Kevin would stand on his head and sing the theme from the TV show *Friends* if you asked him to. You wouldn't have to dare him or pay him or anything.

Jenny Pederson's group went just before ours. Here's what she said.

"Our group did a random survey of 137 River Road School students, and we would like your attention as we report our results."

The Wildcats all groaned, except for Kevin. Jenny, as usual, had to be so perfect. Her group had made a big chart for the presentation, with lots of different colors for the different questions they had asked. She stood in front of her chart like one of those weather ladies on TV and pointed and smiled. WE HATED HER!

"As you can see," she said, "there is a strong preference for dessert items over snacks like popcorn and chips."

Duh, I thought. I knew that even without a big fancy chart. She turned the chart over to the other side.

"We also asked our respondents (*Respondents*— Where did she get that word?) if they preferred cakelike things or cookielike things or candies." She pointed to red, green, and yellow stripes as she talked. They were drawn perfectly, and I knew by whom. Kevin. He loves to make posters and charts, and he always uses rulers and good markers. He'd really decided to join their team. What a traitor.

"We have thought about our survey and our competition and would like to announce . . ."

"Dat-da-da-DAH!" Kevin jumped up with another fancy sign in front of his face.

"Aunt OPAL's Absolutely Luscious Chocolate Chip Cookies!" Jenny cheered. Kevin peeked his head from behind the sign and sneered at the Wildcats and grabbed at his chin the way basketball players do when they want to taunt the other team.

"That's not fair," said Lu, jumping out of his seat. Jenny and Kevin and Tyra and Kelly stood there beaming like they'd just won the lottery or something. "What's not fair?" asked Mr. Harrison.

"That's our idea!" I shouted.

"We didn't know," said Kevin and Jenny together. They had these real fake innocent expressions on their faces, and we just knew they were lying.

"Settle down, boys," Mr. Harrison said. "There are plenty of profits to be made here. There's no rule that says we can't have two chocolate chip cookie companies."

Over our dead bodies. Or theirs.

"Mr. Harrison," Lu said. "We need to change our presentation. Can we make ours after lunch?"

Jenny and Kevin now had these real fake sympathetic looks on their faces. They were gonna pay.

"Sure, boys. But right after recess, okay?"

The Wildcats had an emergency meeting by the dumpsters at recess.

"Who's the big mouth?" I wanted to know.

"Well," said Lu, "we know who walked home together last night."

"Guys!" said Tony R. "He promised he wouldn't tell anyone else. He's supposed to be our friend."

"Them days are over," said Johnny Vang. "For good."

"What are we gonna do for our project?" I worried. I was upset.

"Mr. H has the right idea," said Lu. "We can beat them. We just have to be better."

43

"Yeah, but remember the passes," said Tony R. "If everybody makes chocolate chip cookies, nobody will want them."

"We'll make ours different," Lu said. "Bigger. Fancier. Better than anything Jenny Pederson's ever seen."

We were all inspired by his speech, but what inspired us most was his next idea.

"I know, Wildcats," Lu said. "We'll make 'Wildcat Cookies.' That'll fix 'em."

Yeah, everybody said. That would fix them good.

The war was on!

The Bank Job

NOW THAT WE were in business, it was time to learn about investment. Mr. Harrison had a friend who worked in a bank in downtown St. Paul. His friend arranged for us to come for a tour and talk to some of the people who worked there about their jobs and how they helped businesspeople like us. Can you think of a better place to learn about money than at the bank?

"I hope that this late in the year I don't have to remind you of my expectations," Mr. Harrison said.

He went on to repeat the same old rules we'd heard a hundred times before—every other time we'd gotten to go on a field trip, or even to an assembly. Most of us could say them in our sleep—no loud voices, stay with a partner, you and your partner stay where I can see you. Blah, blah, blah.

The Wildcats had decided that we would fix it so that Kevin didn't have a partner. Lu and Tony R teamed up and so did Johnny Vang and me. That left Tou Vue. We tried to talk him into going with his cousin Blia, but he ruined everything and paired up with Kevin.

"Just keep him away from us," Lu told him.

About 9:30 we piled on the bus and headed downtown to the bank.

The Wildcats live close enough to school that we have to walk every day, so it was a special treat for us to get to ride on the school bus. We ran to the back of the bus and took the seats by the emergency door. Most of the girls sat up front, so Mr. Harrison had the middle to himself. It was a good place for him to be in case there was trouble in either camp. For the most part, things were cool on the bus, though in the back the Wildcats laughed extra loud at any dumb jokes to make Kevin mad. We did that until Mr. Harrison turned around and gave us a dirty look. Then we just sat and talked quietly and looked out the windows.

The bank was in a skyscraper. The bus let us out on a busy street, and Mr. Harrison hurried us inside the first-floor lobby.

Not many of us get to come downtown too often, especially on a school day. In St. Paul the main businesses are on the second floor where the skyways are. The skyways are like bridges between the buildings so that when winter comes, you don't have to walk outside.

"Listen up, gang," Mr. Harrison said. "We will be going up the escalator and then across the skyway. Remember that people are working and shopping and don't want to be bothered by a lot of kids. Try to keep your voices down and stay out of the way."

Tony R and Lu got gleams in their eyes. They both thought of the same plan at the same time.

As we walked across the skyway, the group spread out some. You know how it is, some kids are always in a rush and some kids are slowpokes. Tony R and Lu waited till the group was really scattered and then snuck up next to Kevin. When Mr. Harrison wasn't looking, Tony R distracted Tou Vue, and Lu shoved Kevin. Kevin bumped into an older lady with gray hair and a big pocketbook.

"I beg your pardon, young man!" the lady said.

"Sorry," Kevin said. He got really red in the face, and you could tell he was afraid of the woman.

Mr. Harrison stopped the line and came back to check on the commotion.

"Are there problems back here?" he asked. Before he showed up, Lu and Tony R had already snuck back to their regular places in line. They acted innocent.

"This young man needs to mind where he's going!" the lady with the big purse said.

"Sorry about that, ma'am," Mr. Harrison said. "Kids don't always pay attention, *do they, Kevin?* He didn't hurt you, did he?"

"No," the lady said. "He just startled me. In the future I suggest you keep a better eye on these children."

You could tell that her remark didn't sit too well with Mr. Harrison. He has eyes in the back of his head as it is. Very few teachers keep as good an eye on their students as he does.

"Tell the lady you're sorry, Kevin," he said.

"Sorry," Kevin said.

Kevin didn't tell on us, and we figured he wouldn't. It's a Wildcat thing and a guy thing too. You just don't tell.

The first place we stopped on the bank tour was behind the tellers' windows. It was pretty interesting back there—there was a lot of stuff you can't see when you're out front with your mom while she cashes a check. There were cameras and all kinds of buttons to push in case of a robbery. We talked to one of the tellers—a guy with a big mustache just like Tony R's dad—and he told us that they have to keep track of the money in their drawer to the last penny.

"Have you ever been robbed?" I asked. Some of the kids were nervous, you could tell, in case robbers should come in while we were there.

"The window next to me was held up one time, but I've never been," the teller said. He also pointed out to us that it would be kind of hard to stage a getaway from this location. "We're on the second floor, and there's no place to run or hide. In case any of you guys are thinking about it," he joked.

I don't think any of us were, not even "a certain person."

The next stop on the tour was the vault. That's the room where they lock up the real valuable stuff—like the money, for instance. You should have seen this place! It had walls that were like three feet thick and made out of steel. Superman himself couldn't break into there. Before we went inside, Mr. Harrison's friend—who was an important big shot at the bank—gave us a warning.

"It's very important, boys and girls, that you don't touch anything while we walk through. You might set off an alarm, and it's a nuisance to the security people when one goes off accidentally."

"Don't ruin this, people!" Mr. Harrison said in his most serious voice. We hate it when he calls us *people*, but we know that when he calls us *people*, he means business.

Other than the steel walls and the locks and bars, the vault was kind of a disappointment, especially if you expected to see big stacks of money or gold bars. Mostly the vault contained a lot of small locked closets and drawers and cabinets and safes where the valuable things were kept. There was a table in the middle for writing and counting money, I guess.

"How much money is in here?" Tou Vue asked.

"A couple of million or so," Mr. Harrison's friend said.

"Wow," we said, but the big shot told us that this was nothing. "This is a very small part of what the bank owns. This is just for the day-to-day operation."

"Where's the rest of it?" Tony R asked.

"A lot of it, believe it or not, is in the computer. And there's more at our branch offices and at the Federal Reserve bank."

Mr. Harrison had already told us about the Federal Reserve bank before we came downtown. It's the bank that banks use, and it's run by the government (or something like that).

"If you'll follow me, boys and girls, our next stop is . . ."

Just then a ringing bell went off.

"Uh-oh. I hope no one has broken our rule," the bank guy said.

All of us froze. This could be a major holdup, and someone could get shot!

"Please take the children out into the hallway, Dave," the big shot ordered. Dave was Mr. Harrison's real name.

A woman named Ms. Spencer came to get us and took us into a meeting room. Ms. Spencer told us all about buying stocks and bonds. We tried to pay real close attention because Mr. Harrison had that look on his face that said he was VERY UNHAPPY about our behavior. A few minutes later his friend, the big shot, stuck his head in the door and signaled Mr. Harrison.

Dum-de-dum-dum, we all sang to ourselves.

Then Mr. Harrison opened the door and said, "Excuse me, Ms. Spencer. I need to see Kevin Olsen in the hallway please."

Dum-de-dum-dum-DUM!

Johnny Vang and I were sitting by the door, and we could hear Mr. Harrison out there really giving it to Kevin. It seems that good old Kevin had tried to open one of the drawers in the vault when he thought no one was looking. What Kevin forgot was that the whole place was swarming with cameras, and they had caught him on film red-handed.

Mr. Harrison came back without Kevin. He seemed a little bit calmer, but we could tell he was still unhappy. It was as if there were a pack of hornets swarming around his head. The stocks and bonds lady, Ms. Spencer, finished up by giving us some fake stock certificates we could copy when we got investors for our businesses. They were neat. I could just see the words "Wildcat Cookies" written in calligraphy where the form said "company name."

As you can imagine, the whole class was very low-key on the bus ride home. Kevin did not come with us. For a while we thought maybe he'd been taken straight to the boys' home. Parents were always threatening to send you to the boys' home if you got in trouble. Back at school we found out that Mr. Harrison had called Ms. Filipek-Johnson and asked her to come down to the bank to get Kevin. Mr. Harrison had never been so mad.

"I am very disappointed," he said to us when we got back to school. "I thought we all agreed to be on our best behavior. I guess that's the last time I go anywhere with this class."

He stood there and looked up and down the rows at us. If he was trying to make us feel bad, it was working.

"Does anyone have any suggestions?" he asked. "What I try doesn't seem to work."

Tou Vue raised his hand. "You could make us all miss recess."

Mr. Harrison seemed to be thinking that over.

"Wait a minute," I said. "Why should I miss my recess? I didn't do anything. Mr. Harrison should punish people who cause all the trouble." I felt like I do when Momma puts me on KP because of something Alf did.

"Robert is right," Mr. Harrison said. "That would be unfair. And most of you were terrific, although I did have a report that some other young men in the class were shoving in line."

That stupid Kevin. Now he had turned into a tattletale.

"No, I won't punish you. I want us to end this

year on a high note with your marketplace projects. You know I expect the very best."

We agreed we would give that.

"I do expect the two shovers—and they know who they are—to show enough maturity to own up to their behavior. Other than that, we'll put this day behind us."

Lu and Tony R thought about it all through lunch and most of recess. Finally they knocked on the teachers' lounge door. I followed behind them.

"If it isn't the Gashouse Gang," Mr. Harrison said. He is always talking about the Gashouse Gang and Mutt and Jeff and a lot of other people you never heard of. "I figured I'd see you boys before the day was out. Anything to say for yourselves?"

Lu and Tony R shook their heads and looked at their shoes.

"Eyes up, please." Mr. Harrison always makes you look him in the eye when you are in trouble. "Nothing to say? It's my turn, then. Getting your friends in trouble is not very nice."

"He's not our friend," said Lu.

"Getting anyone into trouble isn't nice. Maybe I should call your dads. Is your dad in the squad car today, Antonio?"

Tony R nodded. He was sniffling too much, and his lip was shaking, and I could tell he was trying to keep from crying.

"I'll tell you what. I'll let you off this time. No

one was hurt, and it wasn't that serious. But I want you to make me a deal. No more problems for the rest of the year. Okay?"

They nodded.

"And it's up to you if you want to be friends with Kevin, but if you decide not to, there will be no feuding in my class. You are to stay away from one another. Is that clear?"

It was clear. We would stay away from him for good. No one wanted a tattletale like him around anyway.

Monsters

THE NEXT ASSIGNMENT for the Wildcat Cookie Company was to come up with a prototype. According to Mr. Harrison, when real businesses think up ideas for new products they create samples first. They make a sample for two reasons, he said. One, they want to find out how much it costs to make their new thingamabob (another Mr. Harrison word) and, two, they want to see if they can convince anyone else to help pay for manufacturing the thingamabob. Those people who give you money to make your new product are called *investors*.

The Wildcats had one major problem on their hands—no one knew exactly what a Wildcat cookie was.

"I thought a Wildcat cookie was just a chocolate chip cookie," I said.

"Duh!" replied Lu. "A chocolate chip cookie is a chocolate chip cookie. Wildcat cookies are special."

"Just for that I won't tell you my other idea," I threatened.

"I bet I know what it is," Lu taunted. "Chocolate chips with nuts, right?"

"You'll just have to beg me. It's a real great one too."

"Okay, Lu," said Tony R. "You cut down everyone else's ideas. What do you think a Wildcat cookie is?"

Lu didn't have a snappy answer to that question. Sometimes Lu thinks he knows everything. Now and then we have to remind him he doesn't.

"Why don't we ask our moms?" I suggested, as innocently as possible. I had a plan, but it would have to wait until later. My suggestion to talk to our mothers sounded like a good idea to the rest of the Wildcats. Actually, it was a good excuse to go walking around the neighborhood from house to house and to avoid doing our homework. Since we were already at Lu's house, we started with his mom. She had just come home from her job. (She's a school secretary but not at River Road.)

"Moms," Lu said. "Moms, what's a Wildcat cookie?"

"Hmm," said Mrs. Underwood. "I think that's something I'd rather not think about."

"No, Moms, this is serious. We need an idea for Wildcat cookies. What do you think they should be?"

"I don't know," said Mrs. Underwood. "I'm partial to butterscotchies myself."

Butterscotchies are an oatmeal cookie with butterscotch chips inside that Lu's Grandma Jackson always brings to Lu's birthday parties. Everybody likes those okay. Maybe they could become Wildcat cookies.

Next we walked over to Tony R's house. His mom stays at home during the day with his two little sisters, who go to kindergarten in the morning.

"*Mami,*" Tony R yelled out to her as went into their house. He calls his mom *Mami*, which, in case you're wondering, is Spanish for "mom."

"Antonio, I hope you boys have wiped your feet. And I hope you are not hungry because I did not get to the store today."

"It's okay, *Mami*, we ate at Lu's house. We have a question for you. What kind of cookies should we make for our store at school?"

Mrs. Rodriguez gave a laugh that sounded like bells tinkling. "You mean what kind of cookies should *I* make for school? *Ay*, every time I turn around the school wants something else."

"No, *Mami*, the Wildcats will make them. We just want to know what kind."

"Well," Mrs. Rodriguez thought. "The wedding cakes I make for Christmas every year are a very easy cookie."

Don't get the wrong idea about those. Mrs. Rodriguez's wedding cakes are not big tall things with a bride and groom on the top. They are little chewy balls full of pieces of nuts.

"You just have to roll the dough into *bolas* and then pop them into the oven. Then, you take them out and roll them in powdered sugar. I suppose you boys could handle that."

"Thanks, *Mami*," Tony R said.

So there was another idea. Wedding cakes could be renamed "Wildcat cookies."

Next stop was Johnny Vang's house. Mrs. Vang was at the kitchen table working hard on her own homework.

"What it is, Mom," Johnny Vang said, and reached up to give her a high five.

"You boys get to play, and the mother is doing the homework. This is not fair."

"We are doing homework," said Lu. "We came to ask you about cookies."

Mrs. Vang gasped. "Xiong knows we do not allow snacks before dinner."

Xiong is Johnny Vang's real name. It sounds almost like John, so Johnny Vang changed his name to Johnny Vang—which he says is a cool American name.

"We don't want to eat cookies," I said. "We want to know what kind of cookies to make."

Johnny Vang's mom laughed. "Cookies were new to me when I came here. Where I come from, we would eat fruit for snacks."

"Fruit! Yuck!" we all said.

"Not yucky. Delicious. Many kinds. Some taste just like candy."

"Mom, what kind of cookies do you like now?" Johnny Vang asked her.

She got up from where she was working and went

to a cupboard. She gave us each a sticky macaroon.

"I like the coconut," she said.

"Me too!" said Lu. He ate his and mine also. Maybe Wildcat cookies could be coconut cookies.

The last stop was my house.

"What a sorry-looking bunch of sailors," Momma said when we came into her house. She had just gotten home from her job out by the airport. She works with computers.

"Guess what our assignment is, Momma? We're asking people about cookies."

"Cookies!" Alf said. He was scooting around on the floor behind one of his toy trucks.

"As the officer on duty, I request a full report," she said.

"My mom likes butterscotch," Lu said.

"Mine likes coconut," said Johnny Vang.

"Mine likes the wedding cakes with lots of nuts," said Tony R.

"Tell the guys about our favorite cookies!" I said. I was so excited I was almost jumping up and down.

"What do you think, Donald?" she asked Alf. "Think we should let these recruits in on the family secret?"

"Cookies!" said Alf.

"What would you mates say if I told you I could make a cookie with coconut (she pointed to Johnny Vang) and with butterscotch (she pointed to Lu) and with nuts (she pointed to Tony R) and with all the chocolate my baby can handle (she gave me a big hug). What would you mates say to that?"

"No way!" they said together.

"Monster cookies!" shouted Alf.

Monster cookies!

"I think we're changing that name, Donald. I think we're calling them 'Wildcat Cookies.' What do you say, sailors?"

"Wildcat cookies!" shouted Alf.

We all loved the idea of Momma's monster cookies—which as you know we planned to call "Wildcat cookies." Momma agreed that, after she picked up Alf from preschool the next day, the guys could come over and she would show us how to make a batch.

The next day the Wildcats arrived armed with their notebooks and calculators, ready to take down the secret recipe.

"Listen up, landlubbers. The key to running a successful galley is organization. Say that with me, men."

"Organization!" we all said.

"As the commander of this ship, it's my duty to assign jobs. Ensign Rodriguez, you are on dry goods. That's the flour, salt, sugar, and baking soda."

"Aye, aye," said Tony R.

"Ensign Vang, you are on dairy. Eggs, butter, milk. Got it?"

"Yes, ma'am," Johnny Vang saluted.

"Ensign Samson, you are on stirring."

"Cool!" I yelled. "That means I get to lick the bowl."

"Not on my watch, sailor. Remember, you're serving the public, and your hands must be scrupulously clean. We don't want to be spreading disease."

"You don't have a job for me," said Lu.

"You, Ensign Underwood, will help Ensign Donald and me with the good stuff." She winked at Lu and pointed to a big bag that we all knew was full of the stuff that makes monster cookies great.

"Ready?" Momma asked.

"Yes, ma'am," we all said.

She plonked a gigantic aluminum bowl on the table. "Okay. We start with the flour. Ensign Rodriguez, put some flour in the bowl."

Tony R stood there for a minute. "How much?" he asked.

Momma looked at him like he was kind of slow. She snatched the big white bag of flour out of his hands and dumped about half of it in the bowl.

"About that much," she said.

"You, Ensign Vang, melt up some of that butter in the microwave." He went to the refrigerator and held up two and then three sticks.

"Whatever you think," she said.

This was how the whole cooking lesson went. We threw in some sugar and then we threw in some eggs and then we threw in some more flour. Then Lu and Alf got to throw in some coconut and some chocolate chips and some Reese's Pieces and some butterscotch chips and some nuts and some raisins and some white chocolate chips and some more of everything they'd already thrown in. At one point Momma announced that she was kind of partial to chocolate chips and grabbed the bag from Alf and dumped all of them in.

Finally we had a big bowl of yellow dough that was loaded up with every kind of treat you could imagine.

"What do you sailors think? Are we ready to start baking?"

It was hard to say. It looked like cookie dough. It was the same color and the same texture when you stirred it. But how could you say?

Momma scooped up a spoonful for herself. Me and Alf got spoons and did the same thing.

"Hmm," the three of us said.

"What do you think, boys?"

She held up the flour.

We shook our heads.

She held up the sugar.

We shook our heads.

She held up the salt.

We nodded.

"But only a pinch," I said. She dropped just a few grains of salt on top of the huge bowl and I stirred them in. Then we each got a fresh spoon and tried it again.

"Perfect!" declared Alf.

"Perfect!" I declared.

"Perfect!" declared Momma. "How about the rest of you sailors? Want to give this cookie dough a taste?"

Lu and Tony R dug right in, but Johnny Vang turned up his nose. He thought raw cookie dough was gross.

"Okay," Momma said, "the next question I have for you personnel is—cookies or bars?"

"Cookies or bars?" Lu asked. "What's the difference?"

Alf and Momma and I laughed like that was real funny.

Alf tugged on Lu's hem. "Cookies are round. Bars are square."

Momma gasped. "That's right, my angel. Give Momma a big hug."

She must have forgotten he was Ensign Donald for a minute there.

"If you're serving a big mess," Momma said, "you probably want to go with your bars. But if you need to be fancier—like if the brass's wives are coming—you may want to make cookies. You sailors aren't having a tea party, are you?"

"Momma, it's for our project at school."

She grabbed a giant square baking pan. "Bars it is," she said and dumped the whole mess on top of it.

"Grab a spatula and start spreading," she ordered.

While the bars were baking, we were assigned a whole set of duties to get the kitchen ship-shape.

"A clean galley is a happy galley," Momma proclaimed, helping us stow everything away. Then we sat around watching the oven, waiting for the bars to be done.

"Mrs. Samson," Tony R asked, "while we're waiting, could you write down the recipe for us so we can figure out how much to invest in our product?"

"Recipe!" Momma said. Then she and Alf and I laughed like hyenas.

"There's no recipe, mate. You just dump your ingredients in the bowl and have a good time."

"But how do you know how much the bars cost?"

"Oh! Cost!" she said. I rolled my eyes.

"Here we go," I said. As you know, cost is something like a magic word for my mom.

Momma fished out of her purse the receipt tape from the cash register at the supermarket. It came streaming out of her purse in a long white ribbon.

"Let see, what do we have here?" She pulled out her hand calculator and punched a few numbers in and scanned the leftover ingredients and punched a few more numbers in. Then she took her pen and did some writing on the receipt tape and circled some of the numbers. She is a whiz with the calculator, and it took her no more than five minutes to figure out the cost.

While the bars cooled, she sat us down and helped us transfer the numbers to our own notebooks.

"You used a fourth of the eggs, three-fourths of the butter. About half the sugar. See—it's all here. And the grand total is $16.89."

"$16.89!" we all shouted.

"Hey, what did you think: food grows on trees?"

"Some of it does," said Johnny Vang.

"Smart sailor," Momma said. "Will that be cash, check, or charge?"

"Say what!?!?!?!" we said.

"Cash, check, or charge? You boys didn't assume this was a charity ship I was running, did you?" she asked.

We all looked at each other.

"Let's get these bars cut," she said. "Then we'll decide where I'm getting my money from! How many bars for your class?"

"Twenty-nine," I said.

"And there are six of us, so we need how many, Donny?"

"Ten!" he shouted.

"That's right, my love, 35. What do you want to do, sailors? Five by seven or six by six?" She scored the knife lightly across the top of the bars so we could see the size of the pieces.

"Five by seven," said Johnny Vang. "They be a little bigger."

"Either way, they aren't very big," said Tony R.

"Five by seven it is," Momma said and proceeded to cut up the bars. "You recruits done the math yet?"

I grabbed the calculator. Like my mother, I love math. "That's almost 50 cents a bar!" I figured out.

"And worth every delicious penny," Momma said, and she and Alf made the noises he makes when something tastes yummy. He and Momma chewed theirs up.

"That's kind of a lot," said Lu.

"And you didn't even add in my profit," said Momma.

"Profit!"

"That's right. Congratulations, gentlemen. You've got your first investor. And as such, I'd sure like to make some money on this deal."

"I don't know," said Lu. "I think 50 cents is too much. If we want a profit, we've got to charge even more."

"Unless . . . ?" Momma prompted.

We all thought about that for a minute.

"We could make them smaller," said Tony R.

Momma nodded.

"We could use less of some ingredients," I said. "Like fewer chips and nuts."

Momma nodded. "But you still want them to be delicious, right?"

We agreed.

"We could make cookies instead of bars!" Johnny Vang said.

Momma nodded.

"We could buy cheaper ingredients," Lu suggested.

That was the only thing Momma didn't agree with. "Believe me, I already buy the cheapest quality I can find."

Momma spent the rest of the afternoon showing us how to use the calculator on her computer and helping us figure out how much to charge for our cookies. We used Mr. Harrison's formula (which she said didn't charge nearly enough for overhead—you know things like the cost of using the oven and renting your mom's baking utensils). Momma estimated that from the same recipe, we could probably make twice as many cookies, and if we added a little more flour and an extra egg, and used a few less handfuls of goodies, we could probably make each individual cookie for 20 cents.

"What I would do," she said, "is I would charge 50 cents each."

"Momma!" I complained. "That's highway robbery."

"A lady's got to make a living," she said.

Eventually we got her to agree to charge 30 cents a cookie, or two for 50 cents. She would be an equal partner, which meant she got one-fifth of any money we made. Her investment was to donate the use of the kitchen.

"And one more thing, sailors. Next time, *you* do all the cooking and all the cleaning up too. Henceforth, this officer is a silent partner. Is that clear?"

"Yes, ma'am," we all said. We wrote up a report on her computer describing our prototype and how much it cost and spent the rest of day enjoying monster, oops, that should be Wildcat cookies!

Business As Usual

MEANWHILE AT SCHOOL, for the most part, it was business as usual. You get in a routine at school. Things pretty much go along the same way every day. This is both a good thing and a bad thing. It's a good thing because most kids—or probably most people, even—don't like surprises. Instead of concentrating on having a good time or learning something, you end up spending your time worrying about what will happen next. That's why there are roller coasters, just so a kid can get himself re-excited every now and then. But you wouldn't want to ride one all day, every day. That would wear you out. The bad thing about routines is that, well . . . they're routine. Everything you do today, you basically did yesterday. It can get kind of boring.

Here is our routine in room 209 (Mr. Harrison's room number). The first half hour or so of the day is the class meeting. After that we have a chance to visit with our friends and get our pencils sharpened. Mr. Harrison calls us to attention and we go through the day's business. This includes taking attendance and collecting any permission slips or parent forms that were sent home the night before. Then Mr. Harrison talks to us about something, like how we should always do our best, or always play fair, or always try to be helpful. This is the part that Lu calls the morning sermon. It's not as bad as it sounds. He doesn't yell or anything, and it never hurts to have a reminder now and then of how to get along in the world. After that it's our turn for announcements or to tell about anything good or bad that happened to us. Most of the kids don't say anything. If there's anything to say, you've already said it to your close friends, and they are the only ones who really need to know. One time Kevin raised his hand and tried to tell a dirty joke for announcements. You can probably guess where he ended up.

After the morning meeting it's time for what Mr. H refers to as *Readin' and Writin'*. (Lu's mom told him at conference time he should pay some attention to *Spellin'* while he was at it.) How

Readin' and Writin' works is Mr. Harrison gives the whole class a short lesson about some problem he sees a lot of kids having in their writing notebooks—like nobody can ever remember where those stupid quotation marks are supposed to go. Then, we get out our notebooks and our individual reading projects and get to work. Some kids read, some kids write, some work on making a project that shows that they read their assigned book. We're all on the honor system usually, though every day Mr. Harrison meets with about ten of us individually to talk about our writing notebooks and to see how we're coming along on whatever book we're reading. Most kids work real hard during Readin' and Writin', and the time goes quickly. At the end of the term, we pick out our best writing and book projects to keep for our portfolios.

Then we go to gym, and we think Mr. H goes to the teachers' lounge and takes a nap.

After gym is math and science time, which goes fast because Mr. Harrison makes it fun. And then we go to lunch, which is also fun.

By then there's only about an hour or so left in the afternoon. That's when we have our economics lessons. Then, if we've had a good day, we usually go out for recess before it's time to go home.

That is the routine, and though you get tired of it some days, everybody usually is okay with it. But you know how it is. Some people just can't help themselves.

Some people have to keep things stirred up. Here's what happened.

We were enjoying the marketplace project very much. We had learned about the stock market and played a game called PIT where you have to scream a lot and trade cards named after commodities like corn and wheat and rye. One day we got to use the good markers and fancy paper to make stock certificates for our company. Wildcat Cookies found two investors besides my mom. Mr. Harrison liked our cookies so much that he put in five dollars. And we also got two dollars from a kid in fifth grade.

We learned about advertising too—about the tricks that companies use to get you to buy their products. Mr. Harrison decorated a plastic bottle with new labels and ribbons and called it Glamorama. We had to get in our groups and come up with a whole ad campaign.

"What is Glamorama for?" Jenny Pederson asked. "Is it shampoo? Furniture polish?"

Mr. Harrison shrugged. "Beats me," he said. "I guess it can be whatever you want. Your job is to sell it, whatever it is."

Great, we thought. Another one of Mr. Harrison's screwball assignments.

"What are we gonna do, guys?" Tou Vue asked the Wildcats. We didn't have to stay in our business groups for this project. We could all be together again. It was great to have the whole group back.

Well, almost the whole group. Kevin was off working by himself.

"I think Glamorama is hair spray," said Lu. None of us liked that idea much. None of us had moms that looked like those hair-spray moms that you see sometimes at the grocery store.

"How about Glamorama deodorant?" I said.

"We all know who needs that," said Tony R.

"If you smell it, it's yours," I responded.

"Everyone knows you can't smell your own," said Tony R. "Of course *you* wouldn't know that."

"Boys," said Mr. Harrison, in his I-better-see-some-work-getting-done-back-there voice.

We finally decided that Glamorama was dog shampoo. The slogan we came up with was "Glamorama: Your Dog Will Thank You." Tou Vue, who we thought was our best artist, drew the dog on the poster. His dog looked sort of like Snoopy, but was a little more goofy-looking around the face because of the big smile he had. Then Tony R and Lu lettered in the slogan, and we drew pictures of flowers over the rest of the poster to show how fresh Glamorama was supposed to smell. The other part of the assignment was to make a commercial. We asked Mr. Harrison if we could bring in a real dog, but he said "absolutely not, no way," so one of us got to be the friendly smelly dog, and since I'm known to be the most frisky (next to Kevin, that is) I got elected to the part. I wore my brown pajamas and stuck some big floppy ears we had cut out of paper to the side of my head.

So here was our commercial. Tony R was the announcer.

"Does this ever happen to you when you walk your dog down the street?"

Johnny Vang walked me around the room on a rope. I was a very friendly and happy dog. Tou Vue and Lu were people walking down the street. They fainted because the dog (me) smelled so bad. Then the dog (me) was sad.

"You should try new Glamorama dog shampoo."

Johnny Vang poured Glamorama all over me. Just confetti—they were going to put some water in the bottle and really douse me, but Mr. H said "absolutely not" to that also. Johnny Vang rubbed the "shampoo" around, and the dog (me) panted and scratched and looked happy again.

"Glamorama is full of all kinds of toxic chemicals and perfumes that can clean up even the stinkiest dog. Even if a skunk gets him. So use Glamorama today. Your dog will thank you."

Johnny Vang walked me across the front of the class again. Lu and Tou Vue petted me.

"What a nice doggy," Tou Vue said.

"And so fresh-smelling too," said Lu.

"Woof, woof, woof," I said. "And thank you!"

Our commercial got probably the third most applause. People really liked Jenny Pederson's commercial. She and Tyra and Kelly had decided that Glamorama was wood softener. (Though now that I think of it, who would buy wood softener?) They used a small wooden table in their commercial. Tyra was the announcer and said that poor Goldilocks could only find one table.

"This table is too hard," said Jenny. She looked pretty funny in a blond wig. Jenny is a Korean girl, and Koreans usually don't have blond hair.

"What you need is Glamorama wood softener."

They pretended to spray Glamorama all over the wood. Then Tyra made a loud grunting noise like in a kung fu movie and karate-kicked the table in half.

"Glamorama," Jenny announced. "It will soften up even the hardest wood."

She wasn't the only one in a wig. The biggest round of applause went to Kevin's commercial. He wore a bathrobe and one of those big, old tall wigs that looked like a beehive. His commercial was for shampoo, and he was the Glamorama Shampoo Girl. For the most part it sounded like those shampoo commercials on TV where ladies talk about how shiny and bouncy their hair is. What made it great was that Kevin used this really silly lady's voice, and the way he walked and batted his eyes was so funny some kids even fell out of their seats. Mr. Harrison laughed so hard, he looked like he was going to cry. We gave

Kevin a big round of applause. His was the last commercial of the day and by far the best.

"That's terrific, Shampoo Girl," Mr. Harrison said. "While the rest of us clean up this room, you go change back into regular Kevin." Then he ordered us to "hop to it!" which means we're supposed to get every speck of paper off the floor so that the janitor doesn't yell at him at the end of the day. It's another part of our routine. As soon as the floor is picked up, we can go out for recess. Because of the garbage left over from the commercials, cleanup took longer than usual. Finally, though, we got everything put away and then waited for Mr. Harrison to line us up to go outside.

"Looks great, guys," he said. He glanced up at the clock. It was five minutes after 2:00. Usually we were outside at 2:00, and Mr. Harrison had his jacket on and looked like he was ready to go too. But we were still sitting there.

"Anyone seen Kevin?" he asked.

Oh. That was the problem.

"You sent him to the bathroom," said Jenny. "About ten minutes ago."

"Great," Mr. Harrison mumbled. He stuck his head out the door and looked up and down the hallway. Then he came and sat back at his desk. He looked furious.

"Want me to go get him?" Lu volunteered.

"Then we'll be waiting for two people."

Nobody said anything for a while. Then the principal knocked on the door. Ms. Filipek-Johnson seemed as upset as Mr. Harrison.

"Does this young lady belong to you?" she asked Mr. Harrison. Kevin still had on his wig and bathrobe and makeup.

"You're holding the class up, Kevin. Where have you been?"

Ms. Filipek-Johnson answered for him. "I found this lovely creature strolling around by the kindergarten. Apparently he's been all over the building in this get-up." Ms. Filipek-Johnson looked both very disgusted and as if she were trying not to laugh.

"Kevin, you were given permission to change clothes. That's all."

Ms. Filipek-Johnson pulled something out of her pocket.

"Kevin showed me this pad of hall passes. He claims you sold them to him for a quarter. I know that can't be true."

Mr. Harrison looked like he wanted to scream at Kevin. All of us wanted to scream at him too. Not only was he wasting our recess, he had stolen those passes, and now he was lying about it on top of everything else and getting our favorite teacher in trouble.

"We'll talk after school," Mr. Harrison said to the principal. He asked her to take Kevin with her for the rest of the day. Which was a good thing. If Mr. Harrison didn't kill Kevin, we would have.

That turned out to be Kevin's last warning. One more problem—any more trips to the office or any more breaking the rules—and the principal told his mother he would have to go to another school.

Spies!

SATURDAY WE DECIDED to meet over in Tony R's
basement and make our advertising posters for
Wildcat cookies. We were allowed to put up five
posters—one poster in the classroom, two in the
hallway where the older kids are, one in the little kids'
hallway, and one in the cafeteria. On the day before
the sale, Ms. Filipek-Johnson would also let each
team read its "radio" commercials on the loudspeaker.

Since it was a Saturday and since guys will be guys,
it took us about two hours to finally get down to
work. We spent a lot of time wrestling around and
playing video games and that sort of thing until Lu
said, "We need to get some work done." So we tried
to focus.

We argued for about an hour over who was the
best artist and what colors we should use on the
posters and what the posters should say. It was kind
of silly when you think about it. The day before, we'd
turned in sample posters to Mr. Harrison, and he had
already approved them, so everything already was
decided. Except for which one of us was the best
artist.

Still, Johnny Vang decided he didn't like green
letters.

And Lu thought tigers were cooler than lynx (which is another name for wildcats).

And I thought up a new slogan: "Cookies so good, they'll make you growl!"

And Tony R liked the old slogan better and wanted to stay with green letters.

Mr. Rodriguez came downstairs and gave us a warning. "*Muchachos*, you have been down here for almost three hours, and I don't see any work. If you want to do well on this project, you had better get busy right now!"

So we did. Tony R and I took turns drawing the big cats in the center of the poster. We worked with the pencils to get the cats just right. Then we got the stencils we had borrowed from Mr. Vang. He had used them to make signs for his new business and said we could borrow them as long as we didn't wreck them. We decided to make two posters with one of the slogans in green letters and two posters with the other slogan in blue letters. The poster with the best wildcat we set aside for the cafeteria. It was just going to say "Buy Wildcat Cookies" in big bold letters.

After everything was all penciled in, we settled down for the easy part—coloring the posters. We put some music on the CD player and spread out around the floor with a couple of boxes of markers. Mostly we didn't talk but just colored and bobbed our heads in time to the music.

One time, when there was this really good rap

song on, I started tapping my marker in time to the beat. Lu had to reach over and grab my hand. It was a good thing he did. Part of my poster was splattered with blue dots!

I fixed it by turning the stray dots into cookies.

Later on, we decided to switch places because it gets boring after a while working on the same thing. Mr. Harrison said the work had to belong to all of us, anyway.

"What was that?" asked Lu.

"What was what?" asked Tony R.

"I heard a noise."

"I think it's just the guys on the song throwing stuff around."

So we colored again for a while.

"I heard it again," said Lu.

We turned off the music and sat real still and listened. Then we heard some giggling and some scratching on glass. There are windows in Tony's basement up high by the ceiling, and that's where the sound was coming from. We looked up.

There they were! It was Kevin, Jenny, Tyra, and Kelly! They were laughing and pointing at our signs and us!

Spies!

They were stealing our ideas.

"Let's get 'em!" I yelled. So we took off up the steps as fast as we could.

"No running in the house, boys," said Mrs.

Rodriguez as we ran by her. "You know the rules."

"Spies!" Tony R yelled at his mom. We kept on running. By the time we got out the door and around to the window they were gone.

"Come on, guys," Johnny Vang said. "Let's get 'em!"

But Tony R held him back. "Be careful," he warned. "They'll probably try something." When you have lived next door to Jenny Pederson as long as he has, you learn to watch your step.

Sure enough, as soon as Lu stuck his head around the side of the house to see where they were, he got blasted with a squirt gun.

"You've got until the count of three," Jenny yelled. "Then we're coming after you."

"Cowards," I hollered.

"ONE," they counted together.

"Eek!" cried Lu.

"TWO!"

"Back to my house," said Tony R. "Fast."

On THREE they let out some sort of a war yodel and were right behind us.

Fortunately, just as we got to the back door, Mr. Rodriguez came out carrying a box to put in the garage.

"Slow down, *slow down*," he said.

When Jenny, Kevin, Kelly, and Tyra saw him, they hid their guns and balloons behind their backs. It was pretty obvious. You could see water dripping down by their heels. As many of us Wildcats as could hid behind Tony R's dad. Good thing he's a big dude.

"Good afternoon, Mr. Rodriguez," Jenny said. "Isn't it a glorious day?" She said *glorious* like it was the longest word in English.

"Good afternoon to you as well, Ms. Pederson. And you are looking glorious yourself, may I say."

We all thought she looked like a dog and that her friends did too.

"We were wondering if Antonio and his friends could come over and play in my yard," she said. She was being so sweet, it made me sick. And all the while she hid behind her back this big old gigantic water gun that could drown a rat!

"I don't see why not," Mr. Rodriguez said. "These boys have worked hard."

"Actually, *Papi*," Tony R said, "we haven't finished our posters yet."

"We know," said Tyra, and they all laughed.

"We should work on *our* posters," said Jenny.

"Hey, girls," Kevin said. He put his arms around Tyra's and Kelly's shoulders. He had a red water balloon in one hand and a yellow one in the other. "I've got a great idea for a slogan. 'Cookies so good they'll make you growl.' "

"Oooooh! You better not!" I warned.

"Let's get to work, gang," Jenny cooed. She fired a couple of rounds of water up over her head as she walked away. It fell on us like rain.

"Hombrecito!" said Mr. Rodriguez. "That's one tough little lady. I'm afraid you gentlemen have your work cut out for you."

The Wildcats stormed back to the basement. We spent about five minutes pounding on pillows and on the floor and saying a lot of bad words. When we calmed down, we started making our plans for getting even.

"We've got to see their posters," cried Lu. "Where does Jenny do her homework?"

"Usually in her bedroom, I think. But I'll bet since Kevin is there, they're probably in the dining room."

"I've got a plan!" Lu announced. Lu always has a plan. Sometimes you wished he didn't. First, he asked if the Pederson's house was set up inside the same as Tony's. Tony R said it was, except opposite, like a mirror image.

"Tony, you go and ring the doorbell. Take Bobby with you. Meanwhile me and Johnny Vang will go around to . . ."

"Why would I be ringing the doorbell?" Tony R asked.

Lu thought about it a minute. Then his eyes lit up. "A peace offering!"

We gathered up all the markers we had already used up on our posters and put them in one box so the markers looked as though they were new. Then we headed over to Jenny's.

While we rang the doorbell, Johnny Vang and Lu went around to the dining room window. The first thing they did was to have an argument about who was going to lift up the other to the window.

"You're too heavy," whispered Johnny Vang.

"Am not."

"Are too."

"Am not."

"Are too."

"Well, you're too short."

"That doesn't matter. We'll be the same height whether I'm on the top or bottom."

"We'll take turns. I'll lift you first."

Jenny answered the front door. "Well, look who's here. Tyra! Kelly! Kevin! Did any of you guys call Ugly Boy Delivery?"

Kevin and Tyra came over and started making faces at us. Kevin tugged his chin to taunt us.

"What do you want?" Jenny asked.

What we wanted to do was beat them up. Instead Tony R put on his real shy smile that he uses around other kids' moms.

"We want to give you a peace offering." He handed her the markers.

"You boys are so nice. We were just getting ready . . ."

Just then we heard a loud scream coming from the side of the house. Johnny Vang came running back around, shaking his hand up and down. "Ow! Ow!

85

Ow! OW! OW!" he cried. He had a mousetrap on his fingers!

"Some people never learn," Jenny said. "Get the balloons, team."

Kevin, Tyra, and Kelly took off, and so did we.

We never did get a look at their stupid posters.

But we did vow we would get even!

Banished

WE REALLY DIDN'T have to worry about getting
even with Kevin. As usual, he ended up fixing himself.

The week before Marketplace Day we put up our
advertising posters. Since Mr. Harrison knew it wasn't
a good idea to have everyone out in the hallways at
the same time, we drew names to see which team got
to put up its posters first. The Wildcats were third,
which was pretty good. There were still a few prime
locations left—like by the gym door and over the
drinking fountain by the principal's office. Each team
had ten minutes to hang its posters. If you weren't
back in ten, one of your posters had to come down.

The Aunt OPAL's (which, by the way, stood for Olsen, Pederson, Allen, and Lee, the last names of the kids in Jenny's group) Absolutely Luscious Chocolate Chip Cookies team had to go last—which seemed a kind of revenge to the Wildcats. Jenny's group's posters ended up on the "fire emergency only" door and places like that. I have to say that their posters were pretty neat. Kevin is a great artist. He had drawn a cute picture of Aunt Opal on each poster. She was a friendly looking grandma lady with white hair and dimpled cheeks. They had used lots of things like glitter glue and fluorescent paint to decorate their posters, and they had even cut out ribbons and lace and other material to paste onto Aunt Opal.

The Wildcat Cookies posters were pretty good too. Ours were much simpler: just a wildcat and a cookie and a slogan. People like simple ads. Mr. Harrison said so.

So what happened was that Jenny, Tyra, Kelly, and Kevin put up their posters around the school. Jenny and the girls came right back, with a minute or two to spare. But there was no sign of Kevin. He didn't come back within ten minutes, and he didn't come back within 20 minutes, and he was still gone 30 minutes later. Mr. Harrison kept right on with what he was doing, which was talking about customer service.

"Who has a bad customer service story?" he asked.

"I do! I do!" I said. "This one time, me and my mom and my little brother, Alf . . ."

"Donald," corrected Mr. Harrison.

"Whatever," I said. "Anyway, so we went to this one restaurant to have dinner, and the hostess wouldn't come over to our table and bring us menus. So my mom finally went and got them herself. Then nobody would come and take our order. So finally my mom got mad and went and said a lot of stuff to the manager. My mom was in the Navy, you know, so she knows a lot of good stuff to say."

The Wildcats all nodded. They had heard my mother say plenty.

Meanwhile, no Kevin.

"That restaurant lost your business," Mr. Harrison said. "And I bet your mother told plenty of other people not to go there too."

"She sure did."

"Who else has a bad story?"

"One time I found a fingernail in my cheeseburger," Tyra said.

"Gross!" everyone yelled.

Mr. Harrison then repeated his instructions about cleanliness and handling food. We had gone on a field trip to a factory over on West 7th and watched how candy was made. It was clean as a pin in there. Everyone wore white uniforms, gloves, and plastic bags on their heads.

"Your bare hands are not to touch anything that

will be eaten. That means from the moment it comes out of the oven or off the stove. Is that clear?"

We all nodded.

Meanwhile, no Kevin.

"Last call for stories," Mr. Harrison said.

Johnny Vang raised his hand. "My friend and I were in this store, and we bought some candy, and I gave the guy a dollar, and he gave me back too much change."

Lu nodded. He was the friend who had been with Johnny Vang.

"Did you give it back?" Mr. Harrison asked.

"He tried to," Lu answered. "But the guy said he never made a mistake."

"Are you sure he made a mistake?"

"I bought two Now-n-Laters and some gum. It should have cost at least 60 cents. Dude give me back three quarters."

"So what did you do?"

"I kept it! I put one quarter in the box they keep on the counter to help sick kids. I kept the rest."

Mr. Harrison laughed. "I know I don't have to remind you boys and girls to be careful with your money. During math tomorrow we'll have another practice on making change. Remember, you're going to have to help the little ones. This is your opportunity to be their teacher."

Just then, who should come tripping into the room but Kevin himself. Mr. Harrison didn't say a word. He just took Kevin by the elbow and walked him back out. He didn't leave us an assignment or anything.

"I was just . . ." Kevin started to say.

"Save it," Mr. Harrison replied.

Much later, after we'd all made up, Kevin told us what had happened.

They walked straight to Ms. Filipek-Johnson's office and walked right in without knocking.

"Our friend here has been AWOL for the last 20 minutes," Mr. Harrison said.

"Kevin!" Ms. Filipek-Johnson said. "I'm calling your mother up here right this minute." She pushed a button on the intercom behind the desk and buzzed the kindergarten room where Ms. Olsen volunteered.

"Miss Hannum, could you ask Ms. Olsen to come up to my office right away?"

When Kevin's mom came she was red in the face both from hurrying, and then, when she saw Kevin and heard what he had been doing, from embarrassment.

"I was only talking to the custodians, Mom. They were telling me how much they liked my posters. I forgot about the time."

"That's the problem with you," Ms. Olsen said. "You forget. You forget your homework. You forget to do your chores. You forget to drop the letters in the mail. I've had it. I don't know what to do."

"I've already restricted all his school privileges,"

Mr. Harrison said. "I don't know what to do, either."

"When's that school store?" Ms. Olsen asked.

"Next Tuesday."

"Maybe he should miss that, as well."

"I don't know," Mr. Harrison said. "Marketplace Day is part of the learning process. I don't believe in making kids miss out on learning."

"But it's fun too," said Ms. Olsen. "The only way he learns is if you keep him away from the fun."

Mr. Harrison shrugged. "It's up to you, I guess. You are his parent." He left them there and came back to the rest of us.

Ms. Olsen made up her mind. Kevin was banished from the marketplace project for good.

"That's not fair!" Jenny Pederson said when Mr. Harrison told her Kevin's punishment.

"Maybe not, but that is his mother's decision."

"I'll give her a piece of my mind," said Jenny.

"You'll do no such thing."

Jenny stormed back and forth, blowing air out of her lips. She was fuming like a steam iron. "Everybody else in here has all their people except for me. I have to risk my grade because of that . . . that . . . mother! It's not fair."

"She's not the one who caused the trouble," Mr. Harrison reminded her. "And you are a very resourceful young woman, Jennifer Pederson. I'm sure you'll figure out a way to make this work." Mr. Harrison raised an eyebrow at Jenny.

It took her a minute, but she got the message.

As we all know, not much gets in the way of Jennifer Pederson and what she wants.

Cookie-Factory Slaves

KEVIN WASN'T ALLOWED to go over to Jenny's anymore, at least not until the end of the economics unit. On Marketplace Day he was not to be allowed in the cafeteria where we had the store. You could tell he wasn't very happy about it. He acted real sad. Or mad. He wouldn't sit with anybody at lunch and mostly walked around with his head down.

On the Saturday before Marketplace Day, the Wildcats met to buy supplies. We got our investment from Lu's dad—who had agreed to be our banker and was holding all our money—and headed over to the big supermarket on West 7th. We grabbed a shopping cart and took off down the aisle. Wouldn't you know the first people we'd run into were Jenny and her crew.

"Hello, boys," she said in a real snotty voice.

"Hello, girls," Lu said back in a voice that mimicked hers.

"They don't give the food away in here, you know," Tyra said. "You have to have money."

"We have plenty of money," I said, "and ours is human money, too, not dog money."

"You say anything else to us and I'll tell the manager you slobbered on the food," said Jenny.

"You just stay out of our way," said Tony R.
"Let's go, gang."

Staying out of each other's way was kind of hard, of course. We were both making cookies, which more or less meant we had to go to the same parts of the store to get our supplies. The Wildcats made a beeline to the dry goods aisle. Jenny, Tyra, and Kelly were right behind us. Our groups were slowed down because we had to comparison shop. That means that rather than automatically grabbing the first bag of flour on the shelves, you have to read the price stickers carefully and figure out which is the best buy. That is harder than it sounds, because packages come in different sizes, and you have to figure out the unit cost—that is the price per pound or whatever. Mr. Harrison taught us a formula in math to use to figure out which product's unit cost is cheaper. Jenny whipped out her calculator and I whipped out mine. It was a battle of the number geniuses. And it was a tie. At the same time we reached for the same brand of flour.

"Your bag has weevils in it," Jenny sneered.

"Your hair has weevils in it," I replied.

"We don't have time to play," said Lu. "Let's go."

So we did the same thing at the sugar and the vanilla. Then we met up again by the frostings and fillings. There were only two bags of chocolate chips! Johnny Vang grabbed both of them.

"You give me those chocolate chips right this

minute, Johnny Vang," Jenny said. She narrowed her eyes shut when she said it, like she was threatening a little kid or something.

"No way, sister," Johnny Vang said in his best street accent. He stuck both packages of chocolate chips behind his back.

"Give them to me. Give them to me! Give them TO ME! GIVE THEM TO ME! NOW!" Jenny started off soft and ended up screaming. "I WANT THOSE CHIPS! GIVE THEM TO US!"

"Back off," Johnny Vang said.

Tyra and Lu got between the two fighters. It looked like Jenny was gonna take a swing at Johnny Vang.

"What is the problem here?" a man shouted.

It was the manager, Mr. Bainbridge.

"Jennifer? Xiong? You're creating a disturbance. What is going on?" He knows most of us by name since we shop here all the time with our parents.

"That boy," Jenny said, pointing to Johnny Vang, "is trying to steal the last two packages of chocolate chips."

"I got money right here," said Johnny Vang, pointing to Lu.

"I know Xiong Vang is no thief," Mr. Bainbridge said. "And as for you, young lady, I've got a whole case of chocolate chips in the stockroom with your name on them. Will that do?"

"That will be fine," said Jenny, all prissy.

Mr. Bainbridge was pretty patient about us making a fuss in his store. A lot of adults would have just thrown a bunch of rowdy kids out the door, but he took us around and helped us find the best prices on the other things we needed.

"You youngsters are almost to the age when I'll be ready to hire you on as stock clerks. You ready for that?"

We nodded. It would be great having jobs and our own money.

When we got to the eggs, he took out a razor, cut the box in two, and handed each group half. That way we wouldn't have any leftovers.

And—the best part of all—he donated to each group a big package of napkins to hand out with our cookies.

"You must put my name on your tables to let people know about our store," he said. We told him we would.

On Monday, when we told Mr. Harrison what a nice man Mr. Bainbridge had been, Mr. Harrison was amused.

"Nice, yes," Mr. Harrison said. "And a smart businessman too."

We carried our bags out of the grocery store (groceries sure are heavy!) and hauled our supplies over to my house. We weren't baking until the next day, so we got kind of bored. When you're bored and you're a Wildcat, there's usually only one thing to do.

You call Kevin. Okay, so boredom was just an excuse. We really missed the guy!!

We figured it was okay to try to make up. After all, he had been thrown off the enemies' team. And we had been friends a long time. And we did sort of miss him.

Tony R made the first call.

"Kevin! How you doing, buddy?"

Kevin hung up on him.

Then Lu tried to call.

"Don't hang up on me. We want to be friends again, okay?"

He hung up on Lu too. Then he hung up on Johnny Vang.

I tried to call him. "We're sorry," I said. I started to hang up on him before he got me, but for some reason I didn't. I waited. I could hear him breathing but he didn't say anything. Finally I said, "Well, bye." He say bye too, and we both hung up at the same time.

"What did you say that for?" Lu asked. "Why should we be sorry? He's the one in trouble."

"I don't know," I said. "We did sort of throw him out of the Wildcats."

"And he sort of got himself thrown out of Marketplace Day. Just like I said he would." Lu is an I-told-you-so kind of guy. Sometimes it makes you sick. We stopped talking about it after that. An argument was about to break out, and we'd already lost one good friend. Well, maybe not. Maybe we'd be back together soon. We would. I just knew it.

On Sunday morning a problem came up that almost sunk us for good. There was some sort of big computer blowup at my mother's job, and at the last minute she got called into work. We asked around and begged and finally hauled everything over to Tony R's house. They have the biggest kitchen, after all, which is the main thing we needed. His mom said a lot of prayers in Spanish when she saw us coming. I guess Lu's mom felt sorry for her, because she agreed to come over and help us out, or at least watch.

We got all our stuff set up and ready to go.

Lu's mom and Tony R's mom, who had been visiting in the front room, came in.

"Who's got the recipe?" Mrs. Underwood asked.

"There is no recipe, Moms," Lu said. "These are Wildcat cookies."

"I beg your pardon," she said.

Johnny Vang jumped in, "It's cool, Moms, you just put some of this in and some of that."

"Oh!" said Mrs. Underwood. "Dump cookies!" She ripped open the tops of our bags of flour and sugar. "Start dumping then. Rosa and I will stand out of your way."

"Caramba!" said Mrs. R.

So we started dumping. At first it was easy, and we thought we'd remembered exactly the right order. Then we got confused.

"Hang on, fellows," Mrs. Underwood said. "I'll let you in on a little secret. Put your dry stuff in this bowl."

We'd already done that.

"Put your wet stuff in this one."

So we did that.

"Save the goodies for last!"

It all came back to us then. The mixing part went fairly well. We got everything together, and the dough looked just the way it had over at my house. Then the mothers tasted it and added some more dry stuff to it and another egg.

"You boys are ready to bake!" Mrs. Underwood announced. "While the oven's warming up, let's clean this good lady's kitchen."

We did, and that took us about a half an hour. We'd been working so far for about two hours, and we still didn't have one cookie to show for it.

"Can we take a break now?" Johnny Vang whined.

"No, no, no," said Mrs. Rodriguez. "You boys have much work to do. Lorraine and I are not baking these cookies."

Then we all whined.

"I'll tell you what," Lu's mom said. "You get two cookie sheets in the oven, get two ready to go, and that will give you about five minutes before you have to repeat the process. Let's go. You're wasting electricity."

After we did what she said, we went outside and

collapsed on the back porch for a few minutes. It sure was hot in that kitchen. Over behind the Pederson's house, Jenny and her crew were also resting on Jenny's porch. They looked as wilted as we were.

"How you guys doing?" I asked.

"Don't ask," said Tyra.

"This is so much work. I can't believe it," said Jenny.

It was one thing to make a dozen cookies or so, but we were both making lots and lots of dozens. Between us, we were making enough cookies to feed a navy.

"Have you guys started on your packaging gimmick yet?" Jenny asked.

"Our what?" I asked.

"You know. Mr. Harrison said that you needed to try to make your product stand out in the store so people will want to buy it."

We had forgotten all about that part!

"Don't worry," Jenny said. "We don't have anything either."

It looked like both groups' gimmicks would be passing out Mr. Bainbridge's napkins with our cookies.

"Boys!" our mothers yelled, and across the yard the girls' mothers yelled, "Girls!"

It was time to rotate the trays. For the next three hours we scooped up cookie dough, plopped it on the trays, spaced the cookies out evenly, opened the oven door, took out one batch, put in another, moved the cookies to the cooling rack, and scooped out some more dough. It was tiring and boring and hot. We had turned into regular cookie-factory slaves.

About 6:00, when we were mostly just walking around like zombies, the cookies were finally done. We were stacking them in bakery boxes when someone knocked on the back door. It was Jenny Pederson. She had a big smile on her face.

"I've got a big surprise," she said. Out from behind her popped Kevin. And his mom.

"What are you doing here?" we asked.

His mom answered. "This sweet young lady decided it would be nice if she could talk my son into breaking his punishment and into thinking of a way to package her cookies."

That sounded like our Jenny.

"I decided it wasn't fair for Kevin to be doing nothing while the rest of us were working so hard," Jenny said.

The mothers looked at each other and rolled their eyes.

Ms. Olsen continued. "I didn't get suspicious until Kevin was on about his tenth picture of Grandma."

"That's Aunt Opal, Mom," Kevin said.

"So I decided that even though a certain young woman . . ."

"That's me," beamed Jenny.

". . . had no business interfering with my son's

punishment—and I will be talking with her mother about that . . ."

Jenny got a scared look on her face.

". . . but her idea wasn't entirely bad. Since Kevin has taken so much of the children's time this year with his antics, he can contribute something back to the group."

"Look," Jenny said. She held up a package of Aunt OPAL's Absolutely Luscious Chocolate Chip Cookies. They were wrapped in red plastic wrap and had a picture of Aunt Opal stuck on top. They looked great.

We were really jealous.

"I knew you guys wouldn't come up with anything, so I made something for you too," Kevin said. He handed Tony R a box full of wildcats made out of tagboard. He had drawn them, cut them out, colored them in, and then looped a piece of orange ribbon through each one.

He showed us how to use them.

"You wrap your cookies in this yellow plastic wrap—like this—and tie the wildcat around the top."

Our cookie packaging looked great too. Different than Jenny's, but just as great.

"Thanks, Kevin," we all said.

"Thank the copy store too," his mother added.

"Can Kevin stay and help us wrap?" Tony R asked.

"Why not?" said Mrs. Rodriguez. "You come in, please, and have a cup of coffee with Lorraine and me."

Kevin's mom agreed.

"I'll help too," said Jenny.

At first we shook our heads, but then we changed our minds. We had a lot of cookies to wrap, and she had, after all, brought our friend back to us.

We put on our plastic gloves and got to work. At the end of the evening, none of us wanted to see another cookie for the rest of our lives.

Money, Money, Money

MARKETPLACE DAY WAS a big success.

"As always!" said Mr. Harrison. Everyone could see how proud he was.

The younger students came to school loaded up with cash—just like we had done when we were in the lower grades. A lot of parents came too. They bought things to take home for family dessert.

Our booth was set up right next to Jenny Pederson's group's. Both teams had the same idea— everyone should come to school dressed alike. Jenny, Tyra, and Kelly wore those old-lady type dresses that are patterned in dots or flowers and have a lot of frills. They had matching bonnets on their heads. The Wildcats wore jeans and our orange and black softball jerseys. It's the closest thing you get to an official Wildcats uniform.

We stuck our Wildcat Cookies posters around our booth, and Tony R and I brought in some stuffed tigers and lions that belong to Alf and to Tony R's sisters. It turns out that wildcats are real popular with little kids. A lot of kids bought Wildcat cookies just because they particularly liked the name or the symbol. Mr. Harrison was completely right about that. Another reason some of the younger boys bought our cookies was because they kind of looked up to the West 7th Wildcats. That was nice too.

We took turns waiting on customers and shopping at the other booths. You could buy fudge and chocolate-covered cherries (I was in heaven), origami, cupcakes, and nachos. Tou Vue and his cousin's group had made jewelry. It sold really well too. One of the other groups of boys made mini-donuts. Making donuts is very messy, so a parent helped them fry. They couldn't make them fast enough. Kids just love those donuts.

And guess what? Aunt OPAL's Absolutely Luscious Chocolate Chip Cookies were actually really good!

By the end of the hour we had sold every single package of Wildcat cookies. There wasn't one crumb left. Some of the little kids made badges out of the wildcat tags. That day there was a whole school full of West 7th Wildcats.

When we returned to class, our next job was to count up our money and see if we'd made a profit. We got out our notebooks with Mr. Harrison's formula and starting counting. We did okay in the money department. We had over $40 to divide among the investors. That meant that my mom, who put in $5, got back around $8.

Jenny Pederson's group sold about the same amount of cookies, but they made more money than us because their cookies cost less to make.

"Yeah, but ours tasted better," I said.

"Tell that to the bank," said Jenny. She always has to have the last word.

Our two groups were hanging around Mr. Harrison's desk waiting for the others to finish counting.

"Can Kevin come back now?" asked Johnny Vang.

"I thought you kids were enjoying a break from him," Mr. Harrison said.

"He's not so bad," said Jenny.

"Why, Jenny Pederson," said Mr. Harrison. "I've noticed you've spent this year competing with him. Now you tell me he's not so bad."

"You're telling me," she said. "He's a good artist. He knows a lot of funny jokes. And he knows how to aim a water balloon."

"How about you boys? What do you think?" Mr. Harrison asked us.

"We think he's learned his lesson," I said.

"For now," Lu added, and then we all laughed.

Mr. Harrison rubbed his chin for a minute. "Sometimes I lose my patience with the boy."

"We know," said Tony R.

"You do?" Mr. Harrison asked. "Do you think I'm too hard on him?"

No one answered that question. We sort of shrugged and looked at one another.

"I don't know, either," said Mr. Harrison. "We've only got a few weeks left. I guess we'll just have to take it one day at a time."

He sounded very relieved at the "only a few weeks" part. But that was okay. We had been a pretty good class as sixth graders go, and everyone knew it. He had been a pretty good teacher. Great, actually. He was nice and fun, and we learned a lot. We had learned a really important thing just that day, as a matter of fact. Teachers don't always know everything, and sometimes they're smart enough to admit it. And that's okay.

"Can we go get him?" Lu asked. "We saved him some treats!"

"You'll have to ask his mom about the treats. Larry and Antonio, you go. And boys, don't let him wander off on the way back. Please."

They promised they wouldn't.

When everybody was done counting, Mr. Harrison announced the results. As you know, the Wildcats didn't make the most money. But neither did Jenny's group, which made it easier to take not being the best. The mini-donut guys made a fortune. They were tired and covered with grease stains and powdered sugar, but they made a fortune. Terry Jones, their leader, got named businessperson of the year.

"Let's talk about those profits," said Mr. Harrison.

We rubbed our hands together in glee.

"Nothing like a room full of 12-year-olds with money to burn," he laughed. None of us kids laughed. Some of us were sort of insulted, actually.

"You know, boys and girls, there's one tradition in the business community we've yet to discuss."

"He means taxes!" said Jenny Pederson, and you could see everyone shoving their money deeper into their pockets.

"No," Mr. Harrison said. "I wasn't talking about taxes, although you're lucky you don't have to worry about paying them. What I'm talking about is philanthropy. Who knows what philanthropy is?"

"I do!" said Kevin. "They're those green bugs that get squashed on your windshield at night!"

"Not quite," said Mr. Harrison. "And welcome back, Kevin. We've missed you. Philanthropy means sharing your good fortune to make the world a better place. I know you're dying to spend that hard-earned money on yourselves. But I'd like you to think about maybe making a donation to someone else. I don't care to whom, and it doesn't have to be much. Just a little from each group."

Mr. Harrison took the donations anonymously. He collected $30 total, and he donated it to the Red Cross in the name of the River Road School, Sixth Grade, Room 209. The kids chose the Red Cross because we always hear about them going in and helping people when there is a flood or a tornado or something.

Then he sprung the best announcement of them all on us.

"What have we here?" he asked. He took out his wallet and an envelope.

"Tickets to Valleyfair!" shouted the mini-donut boys.

"I think you're right," he said. "Hope I have enough. Let's see. Here's one. Two. Three. Four."

"That's enough for us!" yelled the winners.

"Wait. There's more. Five. Six. Seven . . ."

And he kept counting all the way up to 30. He had enough tickets for the whole class!

"Everyone did such a terrific job, I want everybody to go."

The whole class cheered. Even the mini-donut boys. Mr. Harrison promised them they could splash him on the water flume as their prize, and that made them even happier. We scheduled our trip for the last week of school.

And what about Kevin? Well, as I already said, Kevin is Kevin. There were three weeks left of school, which is more than enough time for anything to happen.

"I wouldn't take that kid on another field trip even if I had the military police," Mr. Harrison threatened. He was frustrated again, with plenty of good reasons. Someone sat on a tack, and someone drew a dirty picture in the boys' bathroom, and there was a minor food fight in the cafeteria. Guess who was behind those things?

You're right.

Military police? Mr. Harrison got both, I guess. Tony R's dad and my mom agreed to be chaperones to Valleyfair. Kevin always minds when they are around. Even so, Ms. Olsen came too—just in case.

Valleyfair was great, as always, and there were many fun adventures, but I'll save them for another story. Most of us fell asleep on the bus home. But not Kevin! He still had energy to spare.

Poor Ms. Olsen. Her hair turns whiter every day— even if Mr. Harrison says it's not true that kids give you gray hair.

We think Mr. Harrison turned a little grayer himself this year, now that he mentioned it.